WESTERN ISLES LIBRARIES

WITHDRAWN

Readers are requested to take great care of the item while in their possession, and to point out any defects that they may notice in them to the Librarian.
This item should be returned on or before the latest date stamped below, but an extension of the period of loan may be granted when desired.

Ms Cliff
the Climber

by ALLAN AHLBERG

with pictures by
FRITZ WEGNER

Puffin

Viking

PUFFIN/VIKING

Published by the Penguin Group
Penguin Books Ltd, 27 Wrights Lane, London W8 5TZ, England
Penguin Books USA Inc., 375 Hudson Street, New York, New York 10014, USA
Penguin Books Australia Ltd, Ringwood, Victoria, Australia
Penguin Books Canada Ltd, 10 Alcorn Avenue, Toronto, Ontario, Canada M4V 3B2
Penguin Books (NZ) Ltd, 182–190 Wairau Road, Auckland 10, New Zealand

Penguin Books Ltd, Registered Offices: Harmondsworth, Middlesex, England

First published 1997
1 3 5 7 9 10 8 6 4 2

Printed in Singapore by Imago Publishing

ISBN Paperback 0 14 03.7879 0
ISBN Hardback 0–670–86591–5

Every morning
Clara Cliff gets up.

She puts on her climbing boots,
her climbing clothes
and her climbing hat –

and climbs out of
the window.

In summer and winter,

autumn and spring,

Clara Cliff climbs round the town.

She visits friends, does the shopping

and takes the dog for a walk.

Life has its ups . . . and downs.

Clara and Clifford get on very well.
They agree about everything.
"Cats," says Clara.
"Lovely!" says Clifford.
"West Bromwich Albion," says Clara.
"Great!" says Clifford.
"Fish and chips – and bread
and butter – and mushy peas –
and treacle tart and custard –
and a cup of tea," says Clara.
"Yum, yum!" says Clifford.

Soon wedding bells are ringing.
Clara Cliff takes Clifford Clamber
to be her lawful wedded husband.

Confetti flies,
cameras click,
bridesmaids race around
and feel poorly,

and the happy couple climb off
on their honeymoon.

Time goes by.

Clara and Clifford get a bigger house –
and a play-pen.
Clarissa arrives.

Soon Clarissa starts crawling,
says "Dada!"
and "Me want milk!",

has three birthdays

and goes to playschool.

Life has its downs . . .

. . . and ups!

Then one day the trouble starts.
Clara and Clifford
don't get on at all.
They agree about nothing.

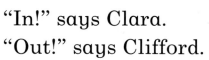

"Up!" says Clara.
"Down!" says Clifford.

"In!" says Clara.
"Out!" says Clifford.

"Chips!" says Clara.
"Pizza – salad – bread and butter –
cup of tea and cake!" says Clifford.

Clara and Clifford
shout a lot,
cry a lot –

and get a divorce. Life has its downs and downs!

Time races by.

In autumn and winter,

summer and spring,

Clara Cliff-Clamber climbs
round the town.

She takes Clarissa to:

school

Brownies

swimming club

shoe shops

piano lessons

skiing lessons

– and discos!

She takes the cat
to the vet,

the dogs
for a walk

and herself
. . . off to bed.

Life has its . . . Z Z Z Z Z Z

Then one day . . .

CLARA
MEETS
CLAUDE!

Clara and Claude get on very well.
"Divorced," says Clara.
"Me too," says Claude.
"Children," says Claude.
"Me too," says Clara.

Soon wedding bells
are ringing,
cameras are clicking
and Clara Cliff-Clamber
takes Claude Clogg
to be her lawful wedded
husband number two.

Time flies!

Clara and Claude mend the play-pen
and get a new pushchair.
Clive arrives.

Clive starts talking,

goes to school

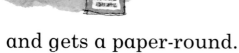

and gets a paper-round.

Clarissa *leaves* school
and gets a job.

And all the while
in summer and autumn,
winter and spring,
Clara Cliff-Clamber-Clogg
climbs round the town.

Life has its ups and downs.
Life has its ins and outs.

Life has its rounds and rounds.
Life has its . . .

...Tangles!

Then one day *Clarissa* . . .

. . . meets Clarence!

(not)
The End